Disney
MOANA

Beware the
Kakamora!

By BILL SCOLLON • Illustrated by the DISNEY STORYBOOK ART TEAM

A special thanks to the wonderful people of the Pacific Islands for inspiring us on this journey as we bring the world of Moana to life.

A Random House PICTUREBACK® Book

Random House 🏠 New York

Sailors fear what the fog may be hiding.
Unseen rocks can rip a canoe apart. Giant waves can swallow
a boat whole. But what they fear the most is . . .

"The Kakamora!" Maui says with a scowl.

"Kaka-what?" Moana asks. She is the daughter of a mighty chief, and she is new to wayfinding.

"Kakamora, Moana," replies the demigod. "Crazy little pirates."

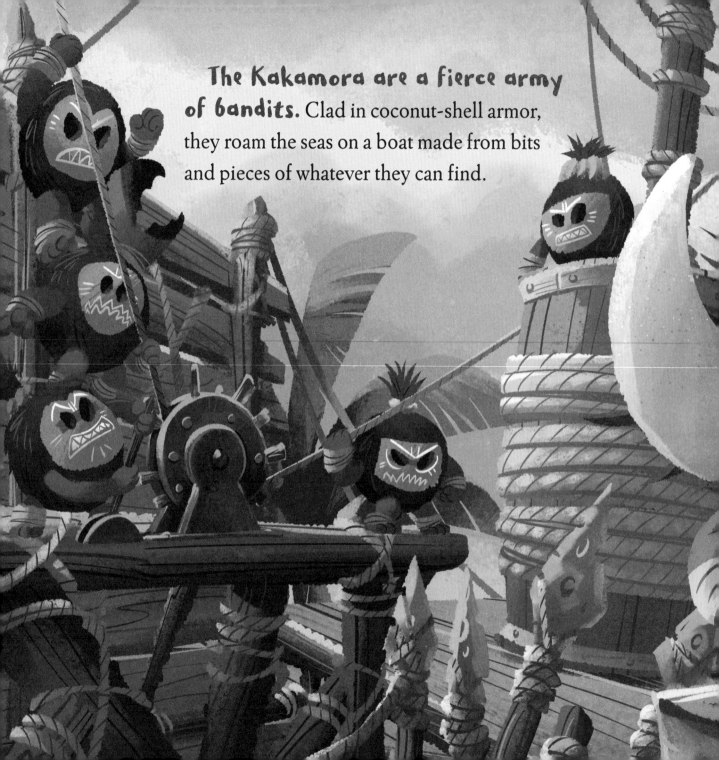

The Kakamora are a fierce army of bandits. Clad in coconut-shell armor, they roam the seas on a boat made from bits and pieces of whatever they can find.

The chief of the Kakamora and his crew
steal from every ship they see.

But there's **one treasure** the Kakamora want **more than anything** . . .

. . . the life-giving heart of Te Fiti!

The Kakamora want its power all to themselves.

Angry war drums fill the air! The pirates prepare to seize Moana's canoe.

BOOM! THUMP-THUMP BRUM-BRUM!

BOOM BOOM BOOM!

The Kakamora attack!

"What do we do, Maui?" asks Moana.

"We run," Maui replies. "Tighten the yard! Bind the stays!"

Suddenly, the Kakamora's massive boat **splits** into **three separate boats!** Moana and Maui are surrounded!

The Kakamora will **stop at nothing** to possess their treasure! As the bandits close in, Heihei the rooster accidentally **swallows the heart!**

BOOM-WHOMP-BOOM-
WHOMP-BOOM-
WHOMPA-BOOM!

But Moana and Maui are on **an important journey** to return the heart to Te Fiti. When they do, the natural balance of the world will return.

"**They took the heart!**" Moana shouts.

BOOM BOOM!
BOOM BOOM!

Maui has just one thing on his mind—**a quick escape!** Moana won't leave the heart of Te Fiti behind, though. Thinking fast, she grabs the oar from Maui's hands.

"Hey, what am I gonna steer with?" exclaims Maui.

SQUAWK!

RATTA-TAT-BOOM!
RATTA-TAT-BOOM!

A Kakamora warrior is about to give the treasure to his chief. Moana swings the oar. She knocks him away and catches Heihei in midair!

Clutching Heihei, Moana **jumps**
back into the canoe.

"Let's go!" yells Moana.
Maui **grabs the oar** and uses
all his strength to steer the boat away.

The Kakamora boats crash into each
other and sink!

Moana and Maui have beaten the Kakamora—
but even greater dangers lie ahead.

BUM-BA RUM-DUM
BUM-BA RUM-DUM!
BLUB-BLUB . . . BLUB!